Fierce Milly
and the
Biggest Conker
Ever

Marilyn McLaughlin   Leonie Shearing

Go Bananas

To Gerry

M.McL.

To Donna and her

little ray of sunshine

L.S.

First published in Great Britain 2003
by Egmont Books Ltd
239 Kensington High Street, London W8 6SA
Text copyright © Marilyn McLaughlin 2003
Illustrations copyright © Leonie Shearing 2003
The author and illustrator have asserted their moral rights
Paperback ISBN 1 4052 0670 5
10 9 8 7 6 5 4 3 2 1
A CIP catalogue record for this title is available from the British Library
Printed in U.A.E.

Contents

Stomp
Stomp
Stomp

Keeping Clean

Me and Billy were out in the garden, keeping clean. That's boring. You can only stand around. We couldn't even go and sit in the Diggings. That's our secret den, where Billy dug a hole big enough for me and him to sit in.

Then we heard Fierce Milly coming up the street. She always pretends to be something loud, like a lawnmower, or a burglar alarm or a helicopter, which gives you plenty of time to hide, if you aren't in a Fierce Milly mood.

Though there's no point really. If she wants you, she just keeps looking until she finds you.

Billy! Susan!

She whacked through our garden gate, stomped up the steps at the bottom, bashed her feet over the gravel on the path.

Billy said, 'I wonder what she's being today?'

'Sounds like a herd of elephants,' I said.

'Hello,' Fierce Milly said, 'I'm a hippopotamus today.'

She's being a very noisy Fierce Milly today.

'There, see,' I whispered to Billy. 'I was nearly right.'

If I'm not right, I'm always nearly right. That goes with being a big sister.

'What are you two doing?' Fierce Milly asked.

'We're keeping clean,' Billy said.

'Who's coming?' Fierce Milly asked.

'Our Auntie Enid,' I said.

'Not the Atomic Kisser! I'm away off.'

Our Auntie Enid is always kissing. She even kissed Fierce Milly. Most people would

be put off by the look of her, but not Auntie Enid. Fierce Milly tried to duck and got the kiss right on her ear. It was loud. It was wet. Fierce Milly went straight home, with her head on one side and her finger in her ear, trying to get the kiss out.

'We've sausage rolls for tea, and chocolate biscuits and pancakes with jam and . . .'

'I'm still away off. I have to find my Slither. He's run away again.'

Here Slither, Slither.

'Yeuch,' I said. 'You are the most disgusting person in the world – having a slug for a pet.'

'Don't you say things about my Slither. He's the fastest slug in the West, and he's my own slug that belongs just to me.'

Fierce Milly's mum doesn't allow her to have pets because she's dangerous to animals and doesn't know how to look after them. So Slither is a secret. She keeps him in her My Little Princess lunch box under her bed, but he keeps escaping.

'You've got to help me look for him.
He's all lost and lonely.'

'We have to keep clean,' I said.

But Billy wasn't listening. He was looking in
all the flowers. 'A green slug! With sticky feet!'

'It's a caterpillar,' I said. 'Everyone
knows that.'

Billy rolled
over an old log. It
was all dusty and
dry underneath,
and he sneezed.

Atchoo!

'Tiny fast tanks!' he yelled.
'Those are woodlice,' I said. Billy
needs a big sister who knows things.

12

Billy heaved over a
stone in the rockery.
'Slugs!' he
yelled.

'Slither!'

Hello, sluggy.

Fierce Milly shouted, picking up
a great big fat black one. 'My lovely
wee Slither. I'd know you anywhere. Look,
he's smiling!'

Found him!

The Biggest Conker Ever

Fierce Milly had Slither in her hand! I stood as far away as possible because slugs are revolting and disgusting and horrible. 'Billy don't you dare touch that slug. You have to keep clean for tea,' I said. But I was too late, Billy was stroking Slither and Fierce Milly was saying, 'He's pleased to see you, give him a kiss,' and then Slither squirted out his eyes the way slugs do, and waggled them at Billy.

'Awwww,' said Billy, 'he's cute.' 'Come away from that slug NOW, Billy,' I said. 'Don't you DARE kiss that slug. Put that slug down. BILLY! Don't bring it near me . . .'

I tripped and fell into a bush. My frock got all dirty and dusty, and it's my best one too. Then I put my hand down on something really sharp and jaggy.

Ouch!

'Waaah! What was that?' I pulled away some old leaves that were lying on the ground.

Billy jumped into the bush beside me.

'Hey, look what Susan's found,' Billy yelled.
'It's the biggest conker in the world.'

'It's mine!' Fierce Milly shouted, and she
put Slither down on a stone and jumped into
the bush too.

'No it's not, it's mine, I found it!' I said.

'You're no good at conkers and I need it
to beat Cecil Nutt. I'm away for string.'

She was right too. Cecil Nutt definitely needed to be beaten at everything, else he got even more bossy.

Billy sat on the ground looking at the conker. It was very, very jaggy.

'I think it's a new sort of conker,' Billy said. 'Probably the biggest conker in the Universe.'

I stood up to get the dust and old leaves off my frock. Then Billy shouted, 'It's got eyes!'

'Stop making things up, Billy,' I said.

'It has a nose and it's wiffling. It has feet. It's walking around – SUSAN!'

'WHAT?' I yelled.

Billy's eyes were enormous. He could hardly speak. 'It ate Slither!' he whispered.

We looked everywhere. No Slither. No conker. Just a little hedgehog licking its lips. It might have been big for a conker, but it was very small for a hedgehog.

Susan, this conker's hungry.

'Awwwww,' I said, 'it's just a baby. Cute, even if it does eat slugs.'

'What'll Fierce Milly do,' Billy asked, 'when she finds out it ate Slither?'

'What will she not do? She's coming. Don't let on!'

Fierce Milly was charging up the garden path waving a long string in the air.

She didn't mind when she saw what had
happened to the conker at all.

'Cool! Now I've got a zoo. One hedgehog.
One slug. Where's Slither?'

Me and Billy looked at each other. I gave
him a Whatever-You-Say-Say-Nothing look.

'Did he go and run away again?' Fierce
Milly said. 'I never knew a faster slug. The
moment my back's turned . . .'

We nodded. That wasn't really telling a lie.
It was just agreeing with Fierce Milly.

'And anyway,' she said, 'now I've got
a hedgehog for a pet, I won't miss Slither
so much.'

What Wicked Did Next

'It's my little hedgehog and he's called Wicked. He's going to live in my bedroom and be my new secret pet. I'll put him on Cecil Nutt's chair at school, and when he sits on him, he'll jump up in the air and hit the ceiling.'

Poor Wicked, I thought. This was terrible – to be squashed by Cecil Nutt's bottom!

23

'Now, what do hedgehogs eat then?' she said. Please don't let her ever find out. I crossed my fingers.

Crisp?

She tried him with half a salt and vinegar crisp. She tried him with one of Billy's chocolate buttons. She tried him with a bit of chewing gum off the bottom of her shoe. Wicked didn't want any of those.

'You always know things, Susan. Why don't you know what hedgehogs eat?' she said.

'Dunno,' I said, helpfully. And then Wicked did something rude.

Pooh wee!

'Yeuch! What's that awful smell?' Fierce
Milly turned round and round, sniffing. 'Was
that you, Billy?'

'No,' Billy said, 'I'd never make a smell
like that!'

'It's Wicked,' I said.

It was too much, even for Fierce Milly.
'Yeuch, that's revolting, that's horrible. You
wicked Wicked.'

We all sat around, holding our noses.

Bad
Wicked!

'You can't keep a smell like that secret, even in your bedroom,' I said.

'I'm not allowed bad smells in my bedroom.'

'Or hedgehogs,' I said.

Fierce Milly looked sad. Wicked wiffled his nose at her.

'I like him, even if he is stinky. He can live in the garden. It can be a safari park. My safari park will be brill because I'll be able to have lots of animals in it.

To Milly
England
From her
Uncle,
Africa

DO NOT
BEND

I'll get my uncle in Africa to post me a hippopotamus and we'll fill up the Diggings with water and it can live in there. And its name will be Mighty Submarine Animal, and we can get a monkey for the tree, and it will be called Magnificent the Monkey. And we'll let Ursula and even Cecil Nutt come and be frightened by everything and smell Wicked.'

Billy said, 'How come it's her safari park and she gets to make up all the names? It's our garden.'

But Fierce Milly was away for the hosepipe. 'Turn the tap on!' Splutter – hiccup – splutter – splash – WHOOSH!

Billy loves hosing. But Fierce Milly wouldn't let him hold the hosepipe.

Billy got cross. 'It's my Diggings, it's my hosepipe, it's my garden!'

'It's my safari park, it's my hippopotamus, my monkey, and my hedgehog!'

Swoosh – SPLASH! Fierce Milly was doing fancy squirting, up in the air, wiggling around. Billy was getting so jealous, he was dangerous.

'Well, your rotten old hedgehog is a rotten old murderer. He ate Slither! So there!'

Oh-oh!

'He murdered my Slither? MURDERED my Slither!'

I tried to get in quick. 'Slither was just his dinner. It wasn't like a real murder. Everything gets eaten by something. Maybe Slither didn't really mind . . .'

But Fierce Milly wasn't listening. First she hosed Billy from top to toe.

'What did I do?' he yelled.

Then she hosed Wicked, the murdering
hedgehog. He rolled up into a tight little ball,
like a conker again.

'Cool,' Fierce Milly said. 'Wish I could
do that, especially when your Auntie Enid
is around.'

You ate my Slither.

Then something terrible happened.

Ouch. His prickles are sharp.

Go, Wicked

Fierce Milly tried to pick up Wicked the conker, to shake him, to see if Slither was rattling around inside. But his spines jagged her hands, and she dropped him and he rolled right into the Diggings. Plop.

He vanished under all
the brown muddy water,
which might be good
for hippopotamuses,
but not for hedgehogs.

The
Diggings
keep Out!

Look out,
Wicked.

'He'll drown!' I yelled. 'Hedgehogs can't swim! Save him!'

Fierce Milly jumped into the Diggings. Splash! Muddy water went all over me. But I didn't care. This was an emergency.

'I'll save you, Wicked. I can swim,' Fierce Milly shouted, though she didn't really need to because the water only came up to her knees.

Then suddenly – pop! Up came Wicked,
swimming round and round the Diggings,
like a little motor boat.

'Hah,' Fierce Milly said. 'Something you
didn't know, Susan Smarty-Pants. You didn't
know hedgehogs could swim, so you didn't.
Go, Wicked!'

But we had a problem. The water wasn't deep enough for Wicked to climb out.

'He can't keep going round and round,' Billy said. 'His batteries will run out.'

I needed to start knowing about things again pretty quickly.

'Hedgehogs don't run on batteries Billy. They're the same as you and me. Animals run on what they eat.'

'Told you Slither was the fastest slug in the West. Look how fast he's making Wicked go!' Fierce Milly said.

I was glad she didn't mind about Slither being Wicked's dinner any more.

Wicked's the best pet ever!

'And I know how to rescue him as well,'
I said. His prickles were too sharp for us to
lift him out with our hands. I went and got
a bucket, and scooped him out. So it was me
who saved Wicked, because I know things.

Billy said that since Wicked could swim,
he could live in the Diggings with the
Mighty Submarine Animal.

Since I was knowing things again, I said,
'No, animals need to live in their own sorts
of places, like slugs like to live under stones in
the garden. And I know where Wicked would
like best to live.'

'Where then?' Billy asked.

'Under the bush, where we found him.'

So we put the bucket
on its side under the bush
and filled it with old
leaves and twigs to be
a wee house for Wicked.
He liked it.

We were all lying on our tummies under
the bush with just our feet sticking out, when
we heard an enormous voice. 'Hello my
dears' and all went quiet. It was Auntie Enid.

Quick, hide!

40

We got to our feet and stood in a row
looking at her. Now for the kissing.

Auntie Enid went sniff, sniff, sniff, and
her nose went all shrivelled.

'What is that awful smell?'

Wicked had done
it again. Auntie Enid
dashed straight
off into the house.
No kissing!

Children, is
that you?

Good one,
Wicked.

Then we dashed into the house, in case there might be sausage rolls.

Mum said we were a disgrace, look at the state of us, and we had to wash and put on dry clothes before there'd be any chance of sausage rolls.

I might as well talk to myself.

Sorry, Mummy.

'Leave some dirt round the edges,' Fierce Milly said, 'in case your Auntie Enid wants to kiss you. It always puts them off.'

So we did that. And it worked! I must remember that again.

We took our sausage rolls outside to see if
Wicked liked pastry or sausage best. But he
was gone.

At bedtime, I said to Billy, 'What a wise
animal Wicked is, to get as far away from
Fierce Milly as possible.'

'But what about the hippopotamus called
the Mighty Submarine Animal and the
monkey called Magnificent the Monkey.'

'We'll worry about them,' I said, 'when
we see them.'

The place where a plant or animal lives is called its habitat. Habitats can be big, like a forest, or small, like a leaf. A habitat provides everything that a plant or animal needs to live.

A frog's home, at the bottom of the garden or in a shady pool, provides shelter and food and helps keep it safe.

Can you spot all the animals in the garden?
Which two animals don't belong in this habitat?

Different animals and plants are found in different habitats. The children wanted to build a safari park in the garden with a hippopotamus in the Diggings and a monkey in the tree. But a garden is the wrong habitat for these animals because it can't provide them with all the things they need.

Next time you're in your garden or local park, look at the plants and animals that are living there. You could turn over plant pots or stones to find creepy-crawlies, or look under a damp bush for snails.
See if you can spot any birds or animals feeding.

Why not start a nature diary? Make a note of the animals and plants you see around you.

Where and when	What	Picture
Saturday: garden	Worms in mud	
Sunday: park	Squirrel in a tree	

The green plants in any habitat can make their own food using the power of the sun. They are called **PRODUCERS**.

Animals can't make their own food and have to get it from plants and other animals. **T**hat's why animals have to move around, looking for their next meal. **T**hey are called **CONSUMERS**.

Some animals, the **PREDATORS**, eat other animals, called **PREY**.

Fierce Milly's food chain shows who is
eating what. Food chains use arrows.
The arrows mean 'is eaten by'.